nickelodeon

pinkfong
BABY SHARK™   WITHDRAWN

Time for School!

HARPER FESTIVAL
An Imprint of HarperCollinsPublishers

Baby Shark woke up with
a smile on his face.
He quickly swam out of bed,
splashing all around.

He ate a big breakfast.

He brushed his teeth.

He was ready to start the day!

IT'S TIME FOR SCHOOL, DOO-DOO-DOO-DOO-DOO-DOO . . .

Mommy and Daddy Shark took him to the bus stop.
Swishing goodbye with his tail, he swam onto the
bus and was quickly on his way.

He could hardly stay still!
Baby Shark had been waiting for the first
day of school, and now it was finally here!

Along the way, Baby Shark spotted some playful crabs.
"Hi!" Baby Shark said. "I'm on my way to school."
"How fun!" Daddy Crab said.
"I always liked art class best," Mommy Crab said.
"I could hold all the crayons with one claw."
Baby Shark laughed.

Then he passed by a big blue whale.
"I'm on my way to school," Baby Shark told him.
"I always liked story time best," the whale said.
"My teacher always read the funniest stories."
"I like funny stories, too!" Baby Shark replied.

The school bus drove past a green turtle next.

"Hello there," Baby Shark said. "I'm on my way to school."

"I made so many friends at school," she told him. "I really learned how to come out of my shell."

Baby Shark smiled. He hoped he would meet friends, too.

Soon the school bus headed into a cave. Baby Shark knew that meant they were almost at the school!

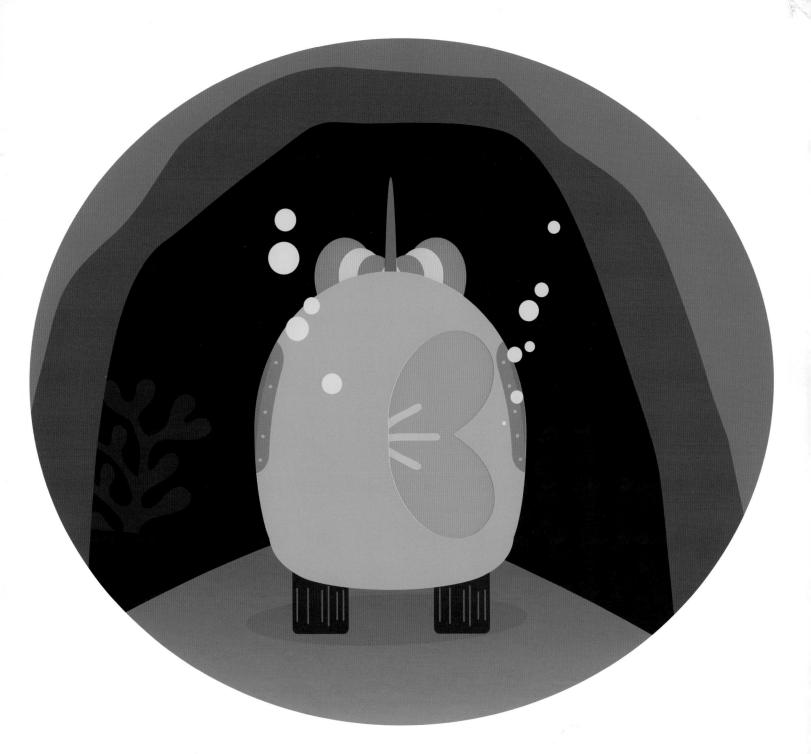

There was only a little bit of ocean left to travel.
But Baby Shark started to get a little nervous.

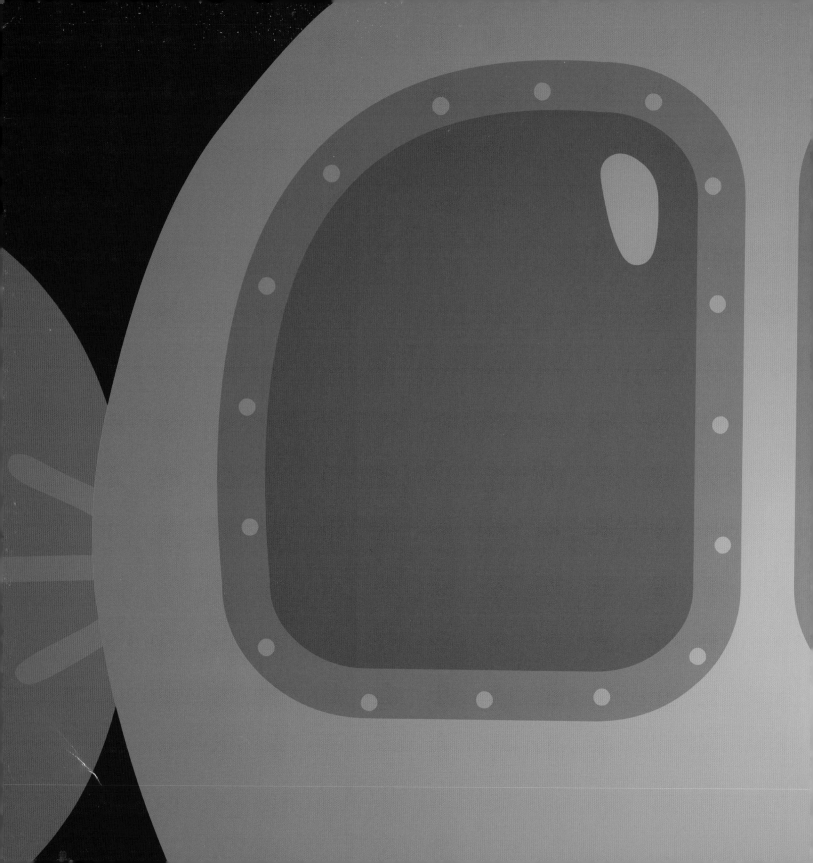

What if I don't like art class? he thought.

Or what if my teacher doesn't read stories that I like?

What if I don't make any friends?

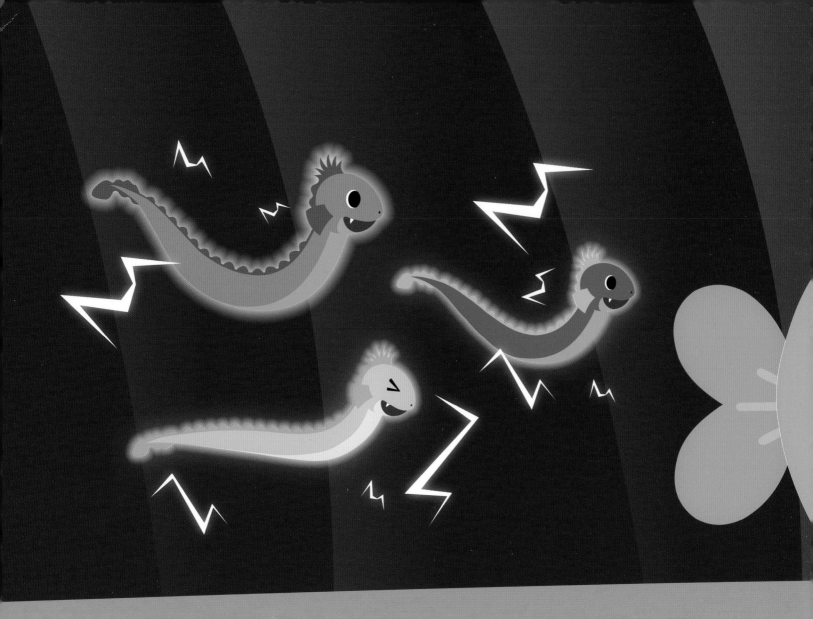

"What's wrong, Baby Shark?" some electric eels asked him.

"I was really excited for school, but now I'm a little scared," he said.

"It's okay to be scared, Baby Shark," they told him.

"Once you get there, you'll find something to be excited about again."

"Maybe you'll go on a treasure hunt and learn about ocean animals you haven't even met yet," a fish said.

"Or maybe you'll do puzzles," a stingray said.

"Or learn math!" a jellyfish said. "I can count with all my tentacles now."

Baby Shark knew they were right. There was something at school for everyone, even Baby Shark.

Vroom! Vroom!

Baby Shark immediately spotted Teacher Shark. "Welcome to school, Baby Shark! We're so happy you're here!" she said.

IT'S TIME FOR SCHOOL, DOO-DOO-DOO-DOO-DOO-DOO!

Daddy Shark and Mommy Shark take Baby Shark to the school bus.

TIME FOR SCHOOL, DOO-DOO-DOO-DOO-DOO-DOO!